The Birthday Queen

by

Audrey and Don Wood

The Blue Sky Press · An Imprint of Scholastic Inc. · New York

JE
WOO
c. 2

THE BLUE SKY PRESS

Text copyright © 2013 by Audrey Wood
Illustrations copyright © 2013 by Don & Audrey Wood
All rights reserved.

Library of Congress catalog card number: 2012045000
ISBN 978-0-545-41474-6

10 9 8 7 6 5 4 3 2 1   13 14 15 16 17
Printed in Malaysia   108   First printing, September 2013
Designed by Kathleen Westray

This book is dedicated to
YOUR
birthday!

The Birthday Queen is always busy
in the Birthday Palace.

There are birthday party invitations
to write and deliver.

Every birthday game must be tested
to make sure it is fun.

When her clowns are invited to parties,
the Birthday Queen must make sure they are funny.
Some are . . .

. . . but others are not.

Today the Queen is preparing for your birthday.

She rushes to the Birthday Palace Bakery,
but the fantastic cake you asked for
is not there.

In the Birthday Palace Kitchen she rolls up
her sleeves. Frosting flies
everywhere.

Now your presents
must be wrapped.

Thank goodness
the Birthday Queen
has three magic wands.

Oh no! It's time for your guests to arrive, and the Birthday Room is not ready!

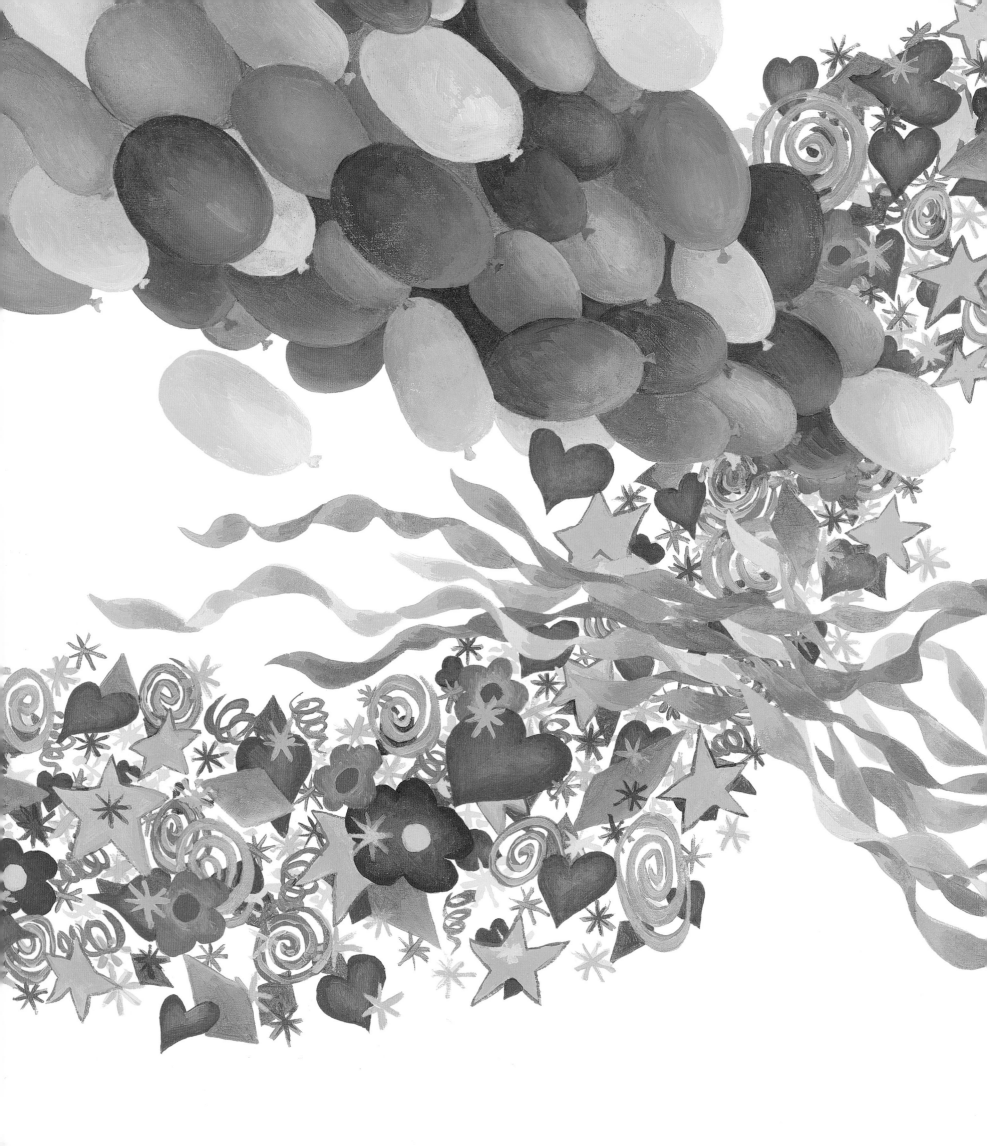

The Queen snaps
her fingers three times.
Balloons, party streamers,
and decorations fly into place.

The doorbell rings. "Let the fun begin!" the Birthday Queen commands as she opens the door. Your guests enter, bearing gifts. Birthday magic is everywhere.

After the games have been played, the Birthday Queen
seats you upon the Birthday Throne.

Then she hurries away.

Your moment has arrived.
The Birthday Queen enters the room.
Your guests clap and cheer. They
have never seen such a cake.

Tapping her Birthday Baton, she leads the singing of your Happy Birthday Song.

After the song, you close your eyes
and blow out all of the candles in
one breath. Your guests go wild.

You open your eyes and see the Birthday Queen standing nearby. She smiles, and when she does . . . she looks just like your mother.